Allan Ahlberg
Treasure Hunt

illustrated by

Gillian Tyler

CANDLEWICK PRESS
CAMBRIDGE, MASSACHUSETTS

Tilly loves treasure hunting.

Each morning

Tilly's mom hides Tilly's breakfast banana

somewhere in the kitchen.

And Tilly hunts for it,

and hunts for it . . .

and *finds* it.

"My treasure!" cries Tilly.

And she eats it up.

After breakfast

Tilly's dad hides

Tilly's rabbit somewhere in the garage.

And Tilly hunts for him,

and hunts for him . . .

and *finds* him.

"My treasure!"

cries Tilly.

And she cuddles

him up.

Sometimes when the snow falls . . .

Tilly's cat hides *herself*

in the garden.

And Tilly hunts for her,

"Here, Kitty!"

And hunts for her . . .

and *finds* her.

"Meow!"

On Tilly's birthday

Tilly's grandma hides

five gold-wrapped coins of

chocolate money somewhere in the house.

And Tilly hunts for them . . .

and hunts for them . . .

and hunts for them . . .

and hunts for them . . .

and hunts for them . . .

and eats them all up.

Sometimes when the
weather is fine Tilly walks
with her mom and dad in the woods.

And *sometimes* her mom and dad
hide *themselves*.

But Tilly just hunts for them . . .

and finds them

right away.

"Easy peasy!" cries Tilly.

Before bedtime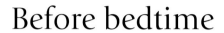

Tilly's dad hides

Tilly's rabbit again,

this time in the garden.

And Tilly hunts for him,

and hunts for him . . .

and *finds* him.

"My treasure!"

cries Tilly.

And she carries

him upstairs.

Then . . . bedtime.

Tilly's mom and dad sit reading the papers.

"Hmm," says Tilly's dad.

"I wonder where Tilly has gone?"

"That's just what I was thinking,"

says Tilly's mom.

So Tilly's mom and dad hunt for Tilly.

And hunt for her,

"Wherever can she be?"

And hunt for her,

"I can't think where to look!"

And hunt for her, "Oh, dear!"

And hunt for her,
up and down
the house . . .

and *find* her.

"My treasure!"

cries Tilly's mom.

"My treasure too!"

cries Tilly's dad.

And they cuddle her up.

for Evie May McGown ~ G.T.

Text copyright © 2002 by Allan Ahlberg
Illustrations copyright © 2002 by Gillian Tyler

First U.S. edition 2002

Library of Congress Cataloging-in-Publication Data

Ahlberg, Allan.
Treasure hunt / Allan Ahlberg ; illustrated by Gillian Tyler.— 1st U.S. ed.
p.   cm.
Summary: After her parents treat Tilly to a treasure hunt, they all play hide-and-seek.
ISBN 0-7636-1542-0
[1. Treasure hunts — Fiction 2. Hide-and-seek — Fiction. 3. Play — Fiction.
4. Parent and child — Fiction.] I. Tyler, Gillian, ill. II. Title.
PZ7.A2688 Tr 2002
[E] — dc21   00-049372

1 2 3 4 5 6 7 8 9 10

Printed in Hong Kong

This book was typeset in Giovanni.
The illustrations were done in watercolor and pen and ink.

Candlewick Press
2067 Massachusetts Avenue
Cambridge, Massachusetts 02140

visit us at www.candlewick.com